The Second-Story Man

Upton Sinclair

Contents

THE SECOND-STORY MAN

BY

Upton Sinclair

THE SECOND-STORY MAN

by UPTON SINCLAIR

CHARACTERS

JIM FARADAY: the second-story man. HARVEY AUSTIN: a lawyer. HELEN AUSTIN: his wife.

SCENE: Library of the Austin home.

Time: 2 A.M.

[The scene shows a luxuriously furnished room. In the centre is a table with a lamp. To the right is the entrance into the front hall, the front door of the house being visible. In the corner is a cabinet of curios. In the rear is a large window opening on the street. Open fire-place. There are two entrances at the left. There are bookshelves, several easy-chairs, etc., in the room.]

[At rise: The stage is empty, and the room is darkened except for the fire in the grate. Sounds of breaking wood are heard at the window.]

JIM. [A roughly-dressed young fellow with a patch over one eye, enters through window, stands gazing about nervously, looks into the hall, etc., then flashes a dark lantern.] This looks pretty good.

[Goes to mantel, takes silver cup and puts it into bag which he carries; then exit left.]

AUSTIN. [Enters at front door without much noise. Hangs up coat and hat, and then stands in entrance. He is a smooth-faced young man in evening dress.] All gone to bed, hey?

[Takes out cigarette case and is about to light one, when a crash is heard off left, as of a vase falling. He starts, then runs to table, opens drawer, takes out revolver, and examines it, and steals off through the other entrance at left, saying, "That noise seemed to come from downstairs."]

JIM. [Enters panic-stricken.] God! What a thing to do! [Gazes into hall and upstairs--long pause.] Don't seem to have waked them.

[Proceeds to examine room, stopping now and then to listen. After placing several articles in bag, he goes to cabinet and tries to open it. This takes some time, and while he is crouching in the shadow, with his back to the entrance right, MRS. AUSTIN appears.]

MRS. AUSTIN. [She is young and beautiful, and wears a night-robe and dressing- gown. She stands looking about anxiously, and then goes to

centre of room, when she hears a sound from JIM, and starts wildly.]
Oh!

JIM. [Leaps to feet, lifting revolver.] Hold up your hands! [She
starts back in terror.] Hold up your hands!

MRS. AUSTIN. [Half complyingly.] I'm not armed.

JIM. Never mind. [Long pause while they stare at each other.] I don't
want to hurt you, lady.

MRS. AUSTIN. [Calmly, after first shock.] No, I suppose not. You only
want to get away.

JIM. That's right!

MRS. AUSTIN. Very well, you may go.

JIM. And you yell for the police the moment I get out of the door,
hey?

MRS. AUSTIN. No, I don't want the police. I don't believe in sending
men to jail.

JIM. Humph!

[Another pause.]

MRS. AUSTIN. Why do you do this?

JIM. It's the way I live.

MRS. AUSTIN. Isn't it a rather trying kind of work?

JIM. It ain't all play, ma'am.

MRS. AUSTIN. [Smiling.] I should think it would be hard on the nerves. [After another pause.] Is there no honest way you can earn a living?

JIM. I don't know. Maybe so. I got tired of looking for it.

MRS. AUSTIN. I might help you if you would let me.

JIM. I ain't asking any help.

MRS. AUSTIN. No, but I'm offering it. [After a pause.] Have you been doing this sort of thing very long?

JIM. No.

MRS. AUSTIN. How long?

JIM. [After hesitation.] This is my first job.

MRS. AUSTIN. What! You don't mean that?

JIM. It happens to be true, ma'am.

MRS. AUSTIN. What made you do it?

JIM. It's a long story.

MRS. AUSTIN. Tell it to me.

JIM. It ain't just a good time for story telling.

MRS. AUSTIN. You are afraid of me? I have no quarrel with you. I don't care anything for the things you have in the bag; and, besides, I suppose you won't take them now. I'm only sorry to see a man going wrong, and I'd like to help if I could. I'll play fair, I give you my word of honor.

JIM. There ain't much honor in this business.

MRS. AUSTIN. No, I suppose not. But you can trust me. Put up that gun and talk to me.

JIM. [Surlily.] It can't do any good.

MRS. AUSTIN. It can't do any harm. Put up that revolver, and tell me what's the matter.

JIM. You'll let me go when I want to? No tricks!

MRS. AUSTIN. I give you my word.

JIM. All right. I'm a fool, I guess, but I'll trust you. [Puts revolver in pocket.] Sit down, ma'am. It must be cold for you. This is a queer kind of layout for a burglar. [Sits opposite her.] You heard that racket I made in the other room?

MRS. AUSTIN. Yes. What was it?

JIM. Some kind of a jar.

MRS. AUSTIN. Oh, my Greek vase. Well, never mind . . . it was an imitation. What were you doing?

JIM. I was looking for something to eat.

MRS. AUSTIN. Oh!

JIM. It would have been the first thing I've had since the day before yesterday.

MRS. AUSTIN. What's the matter?

JIM. No work. [A pause.] I suppose you'll give me the old gag . . . there's plenty of work for a man that's willing.

MRS. AUSTIN. No, I happen to have studied, and I know better than that. Else I should have fainted when I saw you . . . instead of sitting here talking to you . . . . Do you drink?

JIM. Yes, but I didn't use to. Any man would drink . . . that went through what I did.

MRS. AUSTIN. Are you married?

JIM. Yes . . . I was married. My wife is dead.

MRS. AUSTIN. Any children?

JIM. Two. Both dead.

MRS. AUSTIN. Oh!

JIM. It ain't a pretty story, ma'am. It's a poor man's story.

MRS. AUSTIN. Tell it to me.

JIM. All right. It'll spoil your sleep for the rest of the night, I guess, but you can have it. [A pause.] A year ago I was what they call an honest working man. I had a home and a happy family; and I didn't drink any too much, and I did well . . . even if the work was hard. I was in the steel works here in town.

MRS. AUSTIN. [Startled.] The Empire Steel Company?

JIM. Yes. Why?

MRS. AUSTIN. Nothing . . . only I happen to know some people there. Go on.

JIM. It's no child's work there, ma'am. There's an awful lot of accidents . . . more than the world has any idea of. I've seen a man sent to hell in the snapping of a finger. And they don't treat them fair . . . they hush things up. There are things you wouldn't believe if I told them to you.

MRS. AUSTIN. Tell them.

JIM. I've seen a man there get caught in one of the cranes. They stopped the machinery, but they couldn't get him out. They'd have had to take the crane apart, and that would have cost several days, and it was rush time, and the man was only a poor Hunkie, and there was no one to know or care. So they started up the crane, and cut his leg off.

MRS. AUSTIN. Oh, horrible!

JIM. It's the sort of thing you couldn't believe unless you saw it. But I saw it. I didn't care, though. I was a fool. And then my time came.

MRS. AUSTIN. How do you mean?

JIM. A blast furnace blew out, and a piece of slag hit me here, where you see that patch. If it wasn't for the patch you'd see something that would make you sick. It was a pain you couldn't tell about . . . it was a couple of days before I knew where I was. And the first thing when I came to my senses . . . in the hospital, it was . . . there was a lawyer chap with a paper waiting for me.

MRS. AUSTIN. [In agitation.] A lawyer?

JIM. Yes, ma'am. Company representative, you know. And I was to sign the paper . . . it was a receipt for the hospital expenses . . . the operation and all that . . . you see they had to take out what was left of my eye. And of course I couldn't see . . . I had to sign where he told me to. And when I got well, I found they had trapped me into signing a release.

MRS. AUSTIN. A release?

JIM. I had accepted the hospital expenses as a release for all the company owed me. And I couldn't get any damages . . . and my eye was gone, and all the weeks without any wages.

MRS. AUSTIN. My God!

JIM. And they turned me out so weak I could hardly walk; and . . .

MRS. AUSTIN. [Greatly excited.] Who was this man?

JIM. Which?

MRS. AUSTIN. This lawyer?

JIM. I never heard his name. He was a young fellow . . . handsome . . . smooth- faced . . .

MRS. AUSTIN. [Whispering.] Oh!

JIM. Ah, they don't mind it . . . they're smooth. They do that all the time. It's what they get their pay for.

MRS. AUSTIN. [Covering her face with her hands.] Oh, stop!

JIM. What's the matter?

MRS. AUSTIN. [Looking up with white face.] Nothing. Go on.

JIM. It was two months before I could work at all. And the rent came due, and they turned us out . . . it was winter-time, and my wife caught a cold, and it turned to pneumonia, and she died. That's all of that.

MRS. AUSTIN. Go on.

JIM. And then, you see, the panic came . . . and the mills shut down . . . sudden as that. The lawyer told me the company would see I always had a job, but that was only to get me to sign.

MRS. AUSTIN. [Feverishly.] Did you try him?

JIM. I went to the office and tried; but they wouldn't even let me see him.

MRS. AUSTIN. I see. And then?

JIM. Then I went out to look for work. I had the two babies, you know
. . . and God only knows how I loved those babies. I said I'd fight
and win out for their sakes. But Amy . . . she was the little one . .
. she never had been very strong. When you're a poor man, you can't
get the best food, even if you know what it is. It ain't fit milk they
sell for the children in this city; and the baby died . . . I never
knew what was the matter exactly. And there was only one left . . .
and me tramping the streets all day looking for a job. How was I to
take care of him, lady? How could I have helped it? [His voice is
breaking with emotion.] And oh, ma'am, he was the loveliest little
fellow . . . with hair like gold. And so well and strong.

MRS. AUSTIN. [Whispering.] What happened to him?

JIM. A street car killed him.

MRS. AUSTIN. Oh!

JIM. Run over his chest, ma'am. I came home at night, and they told
me, and I near went out of my mind. Can you think what it was to see
him . . . with his eyes starting out of his head like, and his
beautiful little body all mashed flat . . .

MRS. AUSTIN. [Wildly.] Oh, spare me!

JIM. I told you it wouldn't be a pretty story. Do you think maybe you
wouldn't take to drink if you saw a sight like that? [Sinking back.]
Since then I've looked for work, but I haven't cared much. Only
sometimes I've thought I'd like to meet that young lawyer . . .

MRS. AUSTIN. [Starting up.] Oh!

JIM. Yes, it all began with him. But I don't know . . . they'd only jug me. Anyway, tonight I was sitting in a saloon with two fellows that I had met. One of them was a second-story man . . . a fellow that climbs up porches and fire- escapes. And I heard him telling about a haul he'd made, and I said to myself: "There's a job for me . . . I'll be a second-story man." And I tried it . . . but you see I didn't do very well. I'm not good for much, I guess, any more.

AUSTIN. [Enters left, revolver in hand; stands watching, unobserved.] Good heavens!

MRS. AUSTIN. You can't tell. You may have better success than you look for.

JIM. No . . . there's nothing can help me. I'm for the scrap heap.

MRS. AUSTIN. [Eagerly.] Wait and see. You are a man . . . you can be helped yet . . .

AUSTIN. [Coming forward.] What does this mean?

JIM. [Starts wildly and reaches for revolver.] Ha!

AUSTIN. [Raising weapon.] Holdup your hands!

MRS. AUSTIN. [Rushing forward.] No. Stop!

AUSTIN. What do you mean?

MRS. AUSTIN. I say stop! I promised him his freedom!

AUSTIN. My dear . . .

MRS. AUSTIN. Give me the weapon.

AUSTIN. Why . . .

MRS. AUSTIN. Give it to me. [Takes revolver.] Now sit down.

JIM. [Has been staring wildly at AUSTIN.] My God, it's the lawyer fellow!

MRS. AUSTIN. Yes, it is he.

AUSTIN. What does all this mean?

MRS. AUSTIN. Look at this man!

AUSTIN. [Staring.] Why?

MRS. AUSTIN. Don't you know him?

AUSTIN. No.

MRS. AUSTIN. Look carefully. [Turns up light.] Have you never seen him before?

AUSTIN. Never that I can recall. What is his name?

MRS. AUSTIN. I don't know. [To JIM.] What is it?

JIM. Humph! [Hesitating.] He could find out, anyway. Jim Faraday.

AUSTIN. Faraday . . . it sounds familiar.

JIM. [Grimly.] You've served the trick on a good many, I guess.

AUSTIN. [To Mrs. AUSTIN.] What does he mean?

JIM. Don't you remember the Sisters' Hospital? The fellow that had his eye burned out in the big explosion?

AUSTIN. [Startled.] Oh!

JIM. [Sneeringly.] Ah, yes!

AUSTIN. You are the man?

JIM. I'm the man.

MRS. AUSTIN. Harvey, you took this man some paper to sign.

AUSTIN. Yes . . . I remember.

MRS. AUSTIN. Did you tell him what was in it?

AUSTIN. [Hesitates.] Why . . .

MRS. AUSTIN. Answer me, please.

AUSTIN. Why, my dear . . .

MRS. AUSTIN. Did you tell him what was in it?

AUSTIN. But, my dear, it wasn't my business to tell him.

MRS. AUSTIN. Oh!

AUSTIN. I was representing the company.

MRS. AUSTIN, I see.

AUSTIN. It was his place to see what was in it.

MRS. AUSTIN. Harvey! This man with one eye burned out, and not yet over the accident?

AUSTIN. My dear, you don't understand . . .

JIM. [Wildly.] You didn't leave me to find out for myself. You lied to me!

MRS. AUSTIN. At least you permitted him to be misled. You did not tell him the honest truth about the paper, and what would be the effect if he signed it.

AUSTIN. My dear, you do not understand. I could not have done that. I was the representative of the interests of the company.

MRS. AUSTIN. And that is the sort of work you do for them?

AUSTIN. That is the sort of work that has to be done. I cannot help it, much as I would like to . . .

MRS. AUSTIN. [Wildly.] You have done that sort of thing before. And you will do it again!

AUSTIN. My dear . . .

MRS. AUSTIN. And you take money for it! You bring that money home to me! And you never told me how you got it! You make me sharer in your guilt!

AUSTIN. Helen!

MRS. AUSTIN. This was how you earned your promotion! This was what you came to me and boasted about! This was what we married on. This money . . . blood money . . . that you get for cheating this helpless laborer out of his rights . . . out of everything he had in the world!

AUSTIN. My dear, you are out of your mind. You do not understand business.

MRS. AUSTIN. I understand it all . . . a child could understand! It is only you . . . the rising young lawyer . . . that doesn't understand! Harvey, Harvey! Do you know what you have done to this man . . . what you and I together have done to him? We have wrecked his life! We have driven him to hell! We have murdered his wife and his two children. We have turned him into a tramp and a criminal. We have climbed to success on top of him . . . we have made our fortune out of his blood! This house . . . this furniture . . . these pictures . . . all this beauty and comfort . . . all this we have coined out of his tears and agony . . . out of the lives of his sick wife and his two little babies! And you have done this for me . . . you have made me the cause of it . . . you have put the guilt of it upon my young life . . . a thing that I must carry through the world with me until I die!

AUSTIN. [Starting toward her.] Helen!

MRS. AUSTIN. No! Don't touch me! Speak to HIM! It is with him you have to do! What have you to say to him? Don't think about me!

AUSTIN. My dear, be reasonable!

MRS. AUSTIN. What have you to say to him? That is what I want to know! Harvey! Don't you understand it is your character that is up for judgment?

AUSTIN. It can't be as bad as you say.

MRS. AUSTIN. Why can't it? Find out.

AUSTIN. [After a long pause, turns to Jim.] Faraday.

JIM. Well?

AUSTIN. Is what my wife says true?

JIM. It's true.

AUSTIN. You got no damages from the company?

JIM. Didn't you fix it yourself? What do they pay you for?

AUSTIN. And had you no money saved?

JIM. My family had to live on it.

AUSTIN. And didn't you get your job back?

JIM. Until the shut-down, I did.

AUSTIN. Oh, that's so. I forgot that.

JIM. Humph!

AUSTIN. That's too bad. I will have to do something for you.

JIM. Will that bring my wife and babies back to life?

AUSTIN. Oh, your family died! My God . . . that's terrible! [A pause.] Faraday, I can't help that. What can I do? Listen, man . . . you see how unhappy my wife is . . . you don't want to make the thing impossible for me, do you?

JIM. I ain't doing anything.

AUSTIN. Be reasonable, and let me atone for the mistake. We'll say nothing about this . . . about tonight. We'll start over, and I'll see that you get a good job, and a fair chance.

Jim. Humph!

AUSTIN. Will you do that? I'm honestly sorry about it. And perhaps if I can give you some money for a start. .

[Takes out purse.]

JIM. Put up your money. It ain't likely you've got as much there as I'd have got from the company.

AUSTIN. Oh, is that it? Well, maybe that is fair. I'll fix it up with you on that basis.

JIM. And what about the other fellows, hey?

AUSTIN. The other fellows?

JIM. That you've done out the same way you done me. What about Dan Kearney, that lost his life the day after . . and you and the rest of the company sharks fixed it up so that his widow couldn't prove how it was that he got hurt!

MRS. AUSTIN. Harvey!

JIM. Yes, ma'am, they done that. And it ain't the first time they done it, either . . . nor the last. And they've bought juries . . . and judges, too, I reckon . . . there ain't much work of a dirty sort that the Empire Steel Company ain't tried in this city . . . and you can bet their smart young lawyers know all the game! I'm sorry for you, lady . . . you're white, and I'd be glad to help you. But I've seen too much of the company and its ways, and I won't lie down and lick its hand . . . not for any money! I ain't so low I've got the value of my wife and two little babies figured out and ready to hand. I reckon I'll stay on the outside of the fence and take my chances. I'll wind up in jail, I suppose; but there's many a better man than me done the same. So I guess I'll go, and we'll call it off.

[Starts away.]

MRS. AUSTIN. Harvey!

AUSTIN. My dear . . .

MRS. AUSTIN. Is that all you can say to him? You will let him go? [To JIM.] Listen to me. You are right. We can never undo what we have done. We cannot repay you. But at least we must do what we can. We cannot let the evil go on. You yourself have no right to do it . . . you have no right to give up your life.

JIM. I see what you mean, lady; and I'm sorry for you. I'd help you if I could. But it's too late . . . I know that. There can't anybody save me. I'm rotten . . . I'm a boozer. I couldn't stop if I wanted to. And I ain't got any reason to want to. I ain't in the running.

MRS. AUSTIN. [Stretching out her arms.] But what can I do ?

JIM. You can look after them that ain't down. Look after them that
your husband and the rest of the company's sharks will do up tomorrow.

MRS. AUSTIN. No!

JIM. Oh, they'll do it! I know what you mean . . . you'll make him
stop . . . but they'll have another man in his place. It's a machine .
. . it goes right on. Yes, and you won't do as much as you think you
will, either . . . you'll think it over, and you won't go as far as
you mean to now.

MRS. AUSTIN. No! No!

JIM. Ah, but you can't help it . . . you're in the mill, too. It's the
class you belong to. You can talk and feel sorry . . . but you ain't
made to do things. You have to have your houses and your fine dresses
. . . and you couldn't live without them, and there'd be no use your
trying. And that means you have to live off my class . . . you have to
ride on our backs. And it don't much matter which part you ride on, as
far as I can see. You'll make your husband get a new job, maybe; but
he'll do the same thing in another way . . . only you won't find it
out. But any way he gets his money it'll come out of me and my kind.
D'ye see? I do the work . . . I'm the man underneath. I make the good
things, and you get them. [A pause.] Good luck to you.

MRS. AUSTIN. You are cruel.

JIM. Nothing of the kind. I've just told you the facts. I feel sorry
for you. I'd do anything I could for you. [Stretching out his hands.]
See what I've done! I've given you your husband's life.

MRS. AUSTIN. Oh!

JIM. Yes, just that. You've no idea how many times I swore it . . . that I'd kill him on sight . . . that I'd strangle the life out of him, if ever I laid eyes on him again. I used to sit when I was half drunk, and brood over it . . . my God, I even swore it by the body of my little boy! And I've got my gun, and you've taken his away from him. And I don't shoot him. [A pause.] I leave him to you. [Grimly.] You punish him.

[Exit right.]

[AUSTIN stretches out his arms to his wife. She sinks upon the table, burying her head.]

CURTAIN

www.bookjungle.com *email: sales@bookjungle.com fax: 630-214-0564 mail: Book Jungle PO Box 2226 Champaign, IL 61825*

The Codes Of Hammurabi And Moses
W. W. Davies

QTY

The discovery of the Hammurabi Code is one of the greatest achievements of archaeology, and is of paramount interest, not only to the student of the Bible, but also to all those interested in ancient history...

Religion   **ISBN:** *1-59462-338-4*   **Pages:132**
MSRP $12.95

The Theory of Moral Sentiments
Adam Smith

QTY

This work from 1749. contains original theories of conscience amd moral judgment and it is the foundation for systemof morals.

Philosophy **ISBN:** *1-59462-777-0*   **Pages:536**
MSRP $19.95

Jessica's First Prayer
Hesba Stretton

QTY

In a screened and secluded corner of one of the many railway-bridges which span the streets of London there could be seen a few years ago, from five o'clock every morning until half past eight, a tidily set-out coffee-stall, consisting of a trestle and board, upon which stood two large tin cans, with a small fire of charcoal burning under each so as to keep the coffee boiling during the early hours of the morning when the work-people were thronging into the city on their way to their daily toil...

Pages:84

Childrens   **ISBN:** *1-59462-373-2*   *MSRP $9.95*

My Life and Work
Henry Ford

QTY

Henry Ford revolutionized the world with his implementation of mass production for the Model T automobile. Gain valuable business insight into his life and work with his own auto-biography... "We have only started on our development of our country we have not as yet, with all our talk of wonderful progress, done more than scratch the surface. The progress has been wonderful enough but..."

Pages:300

Biographies/   **ISBN:** *1-59462-198-5*   *MSRP $21.95*

The Art of Cross-Examination
Francis Wellman

QTY

I presume it is the experience of every author, after his first book is published upon an important subject, to be almost overwhelmed with a wealth of ideas and illustrations which could readily have been included in his book, and which to his own mind, at least, seem to make a second edition inevitable. Such certainly was the case with me; and when the first edition had reached its sixth impression in five months, I rejoiced to learn that it seemed to my publishers that the book had met with a sufficiently favorable reception to justify a second and considerably enlarged edition. ..

Pages:412

Reference   ISBN: *1-59462-647-2*   *MSRP $19.95*

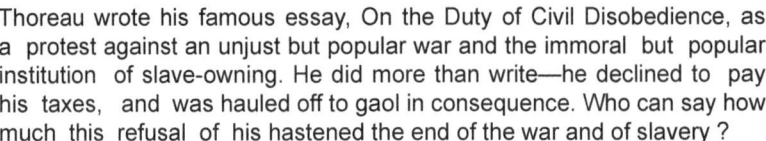

On the Duty of Civil Disobedience
Henry David Thoreau

QTY

Thoreau wrote his famous essay, On the Duty of Civil Disobedience, as a protest against an unjust but popular war and the immoral but popular institution of slave-owning. He did more than write—he declined to pay his taxes, and was hauled off to gaol in consequence. Who can say how much this refusal of his hastened the end of the war and of slavery ?

Law   ISBN: *1-59462-747-9*   **Pages:48**

MSRP $7.45

Dream Psychology Psychoanalysis for Beginners
Sigmund Freud

QTY

Sigmund Freud, born Sigismund Schlomo Freud (May 6, 1856 - September 23, 1939), was a Jewish-Austrian neurologist and psychiatrist who co-founded the psychoanalytic school of psychology. Freud is best known for his theories of the unconscious mind, especially involving the mechanism of repression; his redefinition of sexual desire as mobile and directed towards a wide variety of objects; and his therapeutic techniques, especially his understanding of transference in the therapeutic relationship and the presumed value of dreams as sources of insight into unconscious desires.

Pages:196

Psychology   ISBN: *1-59462-905-6*   *MSRP $15.45*

The Miracle of Right Thought
Orison Swett Marden

QTY

Believe with all of your heart that you will do what you were made to do. When the mind has once formed the habit of holding cheerful, happy, prosperous pictures, it will not be easy to form the opposite habit. It does not matter how improbable or how far away this realization may see, or how dark the prospects may be, if we visualize them as best we can, as vividly as possible, hold tenaciously to them and vigorously struggle to attain them, they will gradually become actualized, realized in the life. But a desire, a longing without endeavor, a yearning abandoned or held indifferently will vanish without realization.

Pages:360

Self Help   ISBN: *1-59462-644-8*   **MSRP $25.45**

The Rosicrucian Cosmo-Conception Mystic Christianity *by Max Heindel* ISBN: *1-59462-188-8* **$38.95**
The Rosicrucian Cosmo-conception is not dogmatic, neither does it appeal to any other authority than the reason of the student. It is: not controversial, but is: sent forth in the, hope that it may help to clear... New Age/Religion Pages 646

Abandonment To Divine Providence *by Jean-Pierre de Caussade* ISBN: *1-59462-228-0* **$25.95**
"The Rev. Jean Pierre de Caussade was one of the most remarkable spiritual writers of the Society of Jesus in France in the 18th Century. His death took place at Toulouse in 1751. His works have gone through many editions and have been republished... Inspirational/Religion Pages 400

Mental Chemistry *by Charles Haanel* ISBN: *1-59462-192-6* **$23.95**
Mental Chemistry allows the change of material conditions by combining and appropriately utilizing the power of the mind. Much like applied chemistry creates something new and unique out of careful combinations of chemicals the mastery of mental chemistry... New Age Pages 354

The Letters of Robert Browning and Elizabeth Barret Barrett 1845-1846 vol II *by Robert Browning and Elizabeth Barrett* ISBN: *1-59462-193-4* **$35.95**
Biographies Pages 596

Gleanings In Genesis (volume I) *by Arthur W. Pink* ISBN: *1-59462-130-6* **$27.45**
Appropriately has Genesis been termed "the seed plot of the Bible" for in it we have, in germ form, almost all of the great doctrines which are afterwards fully developed in the books of Scripture which follow... Religion/Inspirational Pages 420

The Master Key *by L. W. de Laurence* ISBN: *1-59462-001-6* **$30.95**
In no branch of human knowledge has there been a more lively increase of the spirit of research during the past few years than in the study of Psychology, Concentration and Mental Discipline. The requests for authentic lessons in Thought Control, Mental Discipline and... New Age/Business Pages 422

The Lesser Key Of Solomon Goetia *by L. W. de Laurence* ISBN: *1-59462-092-X* **$9.95**
This translation of the first book of the "Lemegton" which is now for the first time made accessible to students of Talismanic Magic was done, after careful collation and edition, from numerous Ancient Manuscripts in Hebrew, Latin, and French... New Age/Occult Pages 92

Rubaiyat Of Omar Khayyam *by Edward Fitzgerald* ISBN:*1-59462-332-5* **$13.95**
Edward Fitzgerald, whom the world has already learned, in spite of his own efforts to remain within the shadow of anonymity, to look upon as one of the rarest poets of the century, was born at Bredfield, in Suffolk, on the 31st of March, 1809. He was the third son of John Purcell... Music Pages 172

Ancient Law *by Henry Maine* ISBN: *1-59462-128-4* **$29.95**
The chief object of the following pages is to indicate some of the earliest ideas of mankind, as they are reflected in Ancient Law, and to point out the relation of those ideas to modern thought. Religiom/History Pages 452

Far-Away Stories *by William J. Locke* ISBN: *1-59462-129-2* **$19.45**
"Good wine needs no bush, but a collection of mixed vintages does. And this book is just such a collection. Some of the stories I do not want to remain buried for ever in the museum files of dead magazine-numbers an author's not unpardonable vanity..." Fiction Pages 272

Life of David Crockett *by David Crockett* ISBN: *1-59462-250-7* **$27.45**
"Colonel David Crockett was one of the most remarkable men of the times in which he lived. Born in humble life, but gifted with a strong will, an indomitable courage, and unremitting perseverance... Biographies/New Age Pages 424

Lip-Reading *by Edward Nitchie* ISBN: *1-59462-206-X* **$25.95**
Edward B. Nitchie, founder of the New York School for the Hard of Hearing, now the Nitchie School of Lip-Reading, Inc, wrote "LIP-READING Principles and Practice". The development and perfecting of this meritorious work on lip-reading was an undertaking... How-to Pages 400

A Handbook of Suggestive Therapeutics, Applied Hypnotism, Psychic Science *by Henry Munro* ISBN: *1-59462-214-0* **$24.95**
Health/New Age/Health/Self-help Pages 376

A Doll's House: and Two Other Plays *by Henrik Ibsen* ISBN: *1-59462-112-8* **$19.95**
Henrik Ibsen created this classic when in revolutionary 1848 Rome. Introducing some striking concepts in playwriting for the realist genre, this play has been studied the world over. Fiction/Classics/Plays 308

The Light of Asia *by sir Edwin Arnold* ISBN: *1-59462-204-3* **$13.95**
In this poetic masterpiece, Edwin Arnold describes the life and teachings of Buddha. The man who was to become known as Buddha to the world was born as Prince Gautama of India but he rejected the worldly riches and abandoned the reigns of power when... Religion/History/Biographies Pages 170

The Complete Works of Guy de Maupassant *by Guy de Maupassant* ISBN: *1-59462-157-8* **$16.95**
"For days and days, nights and nights, I had dreamed of that first kiss which was to consecrate our engagement, and I knew not on what spot I should put my lips..." Fiction/Classics Pages 240

The Art of Cross-Examination *by Francis L. Wellman* ISBN: *1-59462-309-0* **$26.95**
Written by a renowned trial lawyer, Wellman imparts his experience and uses case studies to explain how to use psychology to extract desired information through questioning. How-to/Science/Reference Pages 408

Answered or Unanswered? *by Louisa Vaughan* ISBN: *1-59462-248-5* **$10.95**
Miracles of Faith in China Religion Pages 112

The Edinburgh Lectures on Mental Science (1909) *by Thomas* ISBN: *1-59462-008-3* **$11.95**
This book contains the substance of a course of lectures recently given by the writer in the Queen Street Hail, Edinburgh. Its purpose is to indicate the Natural Principles governing the relation between Mental Action and Material Conditions... New Age/Psychology Pages 148

Ayesha *by H. Rider Haggard* ISBN: *1-59462-301-5* **$24.95**
Verily and indeed it is the unexpected that happens! Probably if there was one person upon the earth from whom the Editor of this, and of a certain previous history, did not expect to hear again... Classics Pages 380

Ayala's Angel *by Anthony Trollope* ISBN: *1-59462-352-X* **$29.95**
The two girls were both pretty, but Lucy who was twenty-one who supposed to be simple and comparatively unattractive, whereas Ayala was credited, as her Bombwhat romantic name might show, with poetic charm and a taste for romance. Ayala when her father died was nineteen... Fiction Pages 484

The American Commonwealth *by James Bryce* ISBN: *1-59462-286-8* **$34.45**
An interpretation of American democratic political theory. It examines political mechanics and society from the perspective of Scotsman James Bryce Politics Pages 572

Stories of the Pilgrims *by Margaret P. Pumphrey* ISBN: *1-59462-116-0* **$17.95**
This book explores pilgrims religious oppression in England as well as their escape to Holland and eventual crossing to America on the Mayflower, and their early days in New England... History Pages 268

QTY

The Fasting Cure *by Sinclair Upton* ISBN: *1-59462-222-1* **$13.95**
In the Cosmopolitan Magazine for May, 1910, and in the Contemporary Review (London) for April, 1910, I published an article dealing with my experiences in fasting. I have written a great many magazine articles, but never one which attracted so much attention... New Age/Self Help/Health Pages 164

Hebrew Astrology *by Sepharial* ISBN: *1-59462-308-2* **$13.45**
In these days of advanced thinking it is a matter of common observation that we have left many of the old landmarks behind and that we are now pressing forward to greater heights and to a wider horizon than that which represented the mind-content of our progenitors... Astrology Pages 144

Thought Vibration or The Law of Attraction in the Thought World ISBN: *1-59462-127-6* **$12.95**
by William Walker Atkinson *Psychology/Religion Pages 144*

Optimism *by Helen Keller* ISBN: *1-59462-108-X* **$15.95**
Helen Keller was blind, deaf, and mute since 19 months old, yet famously learned how to overcome these handicaps, communicate with the world, and spread her lectures promoting optimism. An inspiring read for everyone... Biographies/Inspirational Pages 84

Sara Crewe *by Frances Burnett* ISBN: *1-59462-360-0* **$9.45**
In the first place, Miss Minchin lived in London. Her home was a large, dull, tall one, in a large, dull square, where all the houses were alike, and all the sparrows were alike, and where all the door-knockers made the same heavy sound... Childrens/Classic Pages 88

The Autobiography of Benjamin Franklin *by Benjamin Franklin* ISBN: *1-59462-135-7* **$24.95**
The Autobiography of Benjamin Franklin has probably been more extensively read than any other American historical work, and no other book of its kind has had such ups and downs of fortune. Franklin lived for many years in England, where he was agent... Biographies/History Pages 332

Name	
Email	
Telephone	
Address	
City, State ZIP	

☐ **Credit Card**   ☐ **Check / Money Order**

Credit Card Number	
Expiration Date	
Signature	

Please Mail to: Book Jungle
PO Box 2226
Champaign, IL 61825
or Fax to: 630-214-0564

ORDERING INFORMATION

web*: www.bookjungle.com*
email*: sales@bookjungle.com*
fax*: 630-214-0564*
mail*: Book Jungle PO Box 2226 Champaign, IL 61825*
or PayPal *to sales@bookjungle.com*

Please contact us for bulk discounts

DIRECT-ORDER TERMS

**20% Discount if You Order
Two or More Books**
Free Domestic Shipping!
Accepted: Master Card, Visa,
Discover, American Express

www.ingramcontent.com/pod-product-compliance
Lightning Source LLC
Chambersburg PA
CBHW081204170626
46813CB00009B/3314